Mwar.

THE EVIL PRINCESS

Jennifer L. Holm
vs. Matthew Holm

vs.

THE
BRAVE
KNIGHT

Random House New York

There once lived an Evil Princess and a Brave Knight.

They shared a castle.

They shared a manky cat.

But there were issues.

It was not a very peaceful kingdom.

TRIP!

The Evil Princess wasn't sorry.

That's what an Evil Princess does.

Their Magic Mirror said calm must prevail . . .

and sent them both to their rooms.

She searched her library for inspiration.

Her subjects trembled at her power.

She soon realized it wasn't much fun
being evil by herself.

Meanwhile, the Brave Knight got down to the business of being brave.

He protected the castle.

He battled fierce monsters.

AAAGGHHH!!!!

He soon realized it wasn't much fun
being brave by himself.

Their Magic Mirror said they could come out of their rooms if they promised to play nicely.

It was boring.

It didn't take long to find one.

(Although, honestly, the damsel
was perfectly comfortable.)

The Brave Knight
leapt into action!

He dodged the
hungry dragons
in the moat.

He freed the fair
maiden from her
prison.

And he delivered
her to safety.

That's what a
Brave Knight does!

He wasn't sorry, either.

Their Magic Mirror was not amused.

It didn't seem like a good time to be evil or brave.

They still had to clean up the bathroom.

The Brave Knight volunteered to get fresh towels from the laundry room.

That's what a Brave Knight does!

The Evil Princess knew what she had to do
to restore balance to the kingdom.

And she wasn't sorry.

THE END?

For Millie and Will,
who provided a lot of inspiration for this book
—J.L.H.

For Quintin and Abram:
listen to your parents.
—M.H.

Copyright © 2019 by Jennifer Holm and Matthew Holm

All rights reserved. Published in the United States by Random House Children's Books,
a division of Penguin Random House LLC, New York.

Random House and the colophon are registered trademarks of Penguin Random House LLC.

Visit us on the Web!
rhcbooks.com

Educators and librarians, for a variety of teaching tools, visit us at RHTeachersLibrarians.com

Library of Congress Cataloging-in-Publication Data is available upon request.
ISBN 978-1-5247-7134-8 (trade) — ISBN 978-1-5247-7135-5 (lib. bdg.) — ISBN 978-1-5247-7136-2 (ebook)

The artist used watercolor, pencil, and Adobe Photoshop to create the illustrations for this book.
The text of this book is set in 16-point Schneidler CG.
Book design by Martha Rago

MANUFACTURED IN CHINA

10 9 8 7 6 5 4 3 2
First Edition

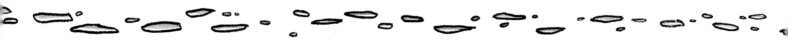